Speci:

I would especially like to thank Dennis Duggan, owner of Air Mango, based out of Montrose and Telluride, Colorado for flying me over the Utah Canyonlands, and his wonderful dog Gretchen, his flying companion. Dennis saved six-year-old Gretchen from certain death at a dog shelter in Colorado. You can see the love Gretchen has for Dennis as she watches his every move and is always ready to join him on a moment's notice to go flying. Dennis has a trailer behind his bicycle so when the two go for excise she can ride in the trailer if she gets tired.

Also a very special thanks to Tracey Napoleone and Gary Knecht, owners of the Canyonlands Needles Outpost & C.N.O. Grill in Monticello, Utah.

I would like to dedicate this book to

Katie Theos, for the wonderful stories

of her father Gus. His adventures as

young man trailing sheep in Western

Colorado and Eastern Utah Canyon

lands till his death in 1986.

Thank you Katie

Chapter 1

Plumping the pillows again, Litsa sat and gazed out the window at the clear Arizona sky. Stars could be seen from horizon to horizon, shimmering in the immense black velvet of an Arizona night. It was warm, too warm for Litsa to sleep, so she leaned back against her pillows, wrapped her arms around her legs, and let her thoughts come to the surface of her mind. Never, in her wildest imaginings, did she ever believe her dream would come true.

It all began when she was very young, maybe five or six years old, she couldn't remember exactly. She would sit on her grandfather Gus' lap before bedtime while he told her the same story for the ten-hundredth time. It was about a lost city somewhere in Utah's Dark Canyon. She never tired of hearing the tale and listening to her Grandfather's voice as he brought it all into near-reality for her young imagination.

Litsa was now a young woman of twenty-eight years and had just completed her degree in nursing at the University of Arizona. She was a striking young woman of Greek descent with long, wavy, dark brown hair and warm brown eyes. Her five foot eight inch frame was attractive and toned from living most of her life outdoors, until college brought her indoors more than she liked. She had no problem drawing interest from the opposite sex,

1

but wasn't obsessed with them by any means. She had dated many young men, but never found anyone she could get serious about.

Now that she was out of school and on her own, it seemed the whole world was hers to explore. Recollections of the past spent with her family and friends filled her mind. She wasn't sure where her nursing career would lead her and was presently exploring various possibilities. She was a country girl educated in the city, and both had their attractions, as well as drawbacks. She had often thought she would like to work on or near an Indian reservation in the West while she was getting her training, but just hadn't made a firm decision yet. As she pondered this prospect once again, trying to imagine herself in a nursing environment in some hospital she had never seen, the phone rang, shaking her back to reality.

"Litsa, you need to come home right away," her mother Sophia said, softly. "Your grandfather has had a heart attack and is in the hospital. When you get your flight information call me and I'll meet you at the airport. They are watching him very closely. Surgery is imminent. He has been asking for you."

Litsa couldn't believe what she heard and mumbled some reply to her mother while her mind flew in ten directions at once. Her grandfather had always been big and strong, her hero, her strength, and now he lay in a hospital bed, maybe dying. Grandfather Gus had always been the picture of health, even though old age had made its presence known. He was a dynamic man, so full of life and kindness. Through her tears, Litsa called the airline and made a reservation for taking the next flight out to Grand Junction, Colorado.

She couldn't get a flight out until early morning, so she stayed up all night packing and pacing the floor. She called her mother nearly every hour to see how her grandfather was doing. He was in ICU, but holding his own her mother had told her. Images of him crowded into her mind. He was laughing at her childhood antics, wiping away her tears, holding her hand as they walked, teaching her about the world, and sharing stories about his life. She hugged herself remembering his hugs and how his voice sounded while her heart ached beyond belief. Fear planted itself firmly in her stomach, like a boulder of granite. She managed to drink a cup of chamomile tea to help calm her nerves.

Finally dawn found her boarding her flight. It seemed as if the plane was crawling across the sky. Time stood still as she tried to get control over the myriad of emotions she was experiencing through the memories of this man she adored and cherished. The possibility of losing her grandfather so overwhelmed her she didn't notice she'd been crying most of the flight.

When she landed, her mother was waiting at the airport. Rushing into her mother's arms she cried, "Oh Mother, I can't bear the thought of losing him. He is the best friend I've ever had." Her mother tried to comfort her as they walked to the car. Sophia was always the strong one in the family, and the one to calm Litsa down.

"Try to get a hold on yourself, Litsa," Sophia said firmly as they left the airport. "He needs your strength as well as your love."

On the ride to the hospital, her mind was again filled with memories of the long summer days in the high country of Colorado, and the dark nights at the desert camps in Utah, where a good fire and coffee with lots of sugar made listening to his magical stories fun and exhilarating.

"I just can't stand the thought of him lying in that hospital," Litsa said, trying to hold back the tears. She jumped from the car the moment it stopped in the visitors' parking spot and ran into the hospital, pausing at the admitting desk only long enough to find out what room he was in.

"Second floor, room 205," the admitting clerk told her adding, "and only family is allowed to see him."

Litsa waved her hand and called back, "Grand-daughter," as she sped toward the elevator looking over her shoulder at her mother trailing behind. She waved and hit the button for the second floor. The elevator dragged itself up slowly. Litsa tapped her foot impatiently and time seemed to stand still once again. When the door opened, signs on the wall opposite indicated which way to turn to get to room 205.

Outside the room she paused to gather herself together and catch her breath before entering. She didn't want Grandfather to see her tears or how she was shaking. He needs me to be strong, she told herself silently. With a deep breath she opened the door. His eyes were closed as she tiptoed into the room closing the door silently after waving down the hall to her mother.

He had IV's running out of both arms and he was so pale that her heart felt as though it would break seeing him lying there so helpless. She stepped quietly over to the side of his bed and leaned over to kiss his forehead. As she did, he opened his eyes and managed a weak smile.

"Ahh, Litsa, it's good to see you," he whispered hoarsely.

"Shhhh," she said placing her finger on his lips. "Don't try to talk, Grandfather." She took his time-withered hand in hers and fought back the tears.

"Litsa, I have something I must tell you", Gus said.

"It can wait", Litsa said. "You must save your energy."

"No, no, I must tell you now. It's a secret, so come close so I can whisper it to you," Gus said squeezing her hand slightly. She leaned close, but it was difficult to hear him with all the machines that were monitoring his condition

4

beeping and whirring. When she was finally able to understand what he was saying it made her jump back, eyes wide with surprise.

"Promise me you will do as I tell you," he said. As she nodded solemnly, he reached into the drawer in his tray and withdrew something. He placed it into Litsa's hand and said, "Take this, you will need to have it with you." As she opened her hand she saw it was a small, oddly shaped piece of gold. Her questioning eyes met his and he nodded and smiled.

A moment later her mother and a nurse entered the room. "I'm sorry to interrupt your visit, but you will have to leave for a few minutes," the nurse told Litsa and her mother. "I need to check his blood pressure and tubes," she smiled.

Out in the hall Litsa told her mother, "You look exhausted. If you want to go home and get some rest, I'll stay here with him. If there's any change in his condition I'll call you."

"I could use a little sleep, but I'll be back in a few hours," her mother yawned." Call me the minute there is anything to report," she said hugging Litsa. Then she was walking back down the hall.

The day wore on and Gus slept peacefully except for the interruptions by the duty nurse each time they needed to check his IV's and take his vital signs. It seemed he was no longer aware she was in the room, or if he was he was saving his energy as she had urged him. On a small table there were two floral arrangements lending their gentle fragrances to the stagnant air of the room. She was glad for the color they offered, a bit of brightness in an otherwise bleak décor.

The nursing and lab staff was pleasant and fostered a positive and cheerful aura, filling Litsa with a sense of hope. She had told a couple of the nurses that she, too, was a nurse, and they chatted amiably with her while

5

they went about their duties. Grandfather slept on, but his vital signs were good and his color was gradually improving.

"I would like to stay here through the night," Litsa told the evening nurse. "I'm a nurse. I'll just stay here and keep an eye on him."

"I saw a note to that affect," the nurse smiled. "I'll have to check with the doctor, but I think that will be alright," she said as she checked the IV's. After taking Gus' vital signs she nodded to Litsa saying, "I'll just give his doctor a call to authorize you to stay with him."

Gus opened his eyes after the nurse had left the room and smiled at Litsa. "You're a good girl," he winked. "I knew you'd come and give me strength. You're very special," and he gave her hand a squeeze. He then told her more about their secret, filling in some details he couldn't convey earlier. He was feeling better, he said. He asked her again to keep their secret to herself and to follow his directions, then closed his eyes and went to sleep again. Litsa sat by his side all night, never once leaving him alone, thinking about all he had imparted to her.

The following day Gus was taken to surgery for a triple bypass. Litsa and her mother had been with him briefly before he was taken to pre-op and were uplifted by his improvement in the past twenty-four hours. The nurse had told them he was doing remarkably well and the surgery should go as well. They sat in a waiting area drinking tea and silently praying while the time dragged on. After four hours in the operating room the doctor came out to them smiling. He shook their hands and told them Gus had done very well in surgery and was in recovery. They both emitted huge sighs of relief and hugged the doctor, then each other. Litsa knew he would recover from that moment on, but had felt assurance even before the surgery. She knew he wanted to continue his life and had accepted her energy and hope as a means.

Chapter 2

Sheep ranching was a common way of life on the western slopes of the Rocky Mountains along the Utah border. The ways of these people were difficult at times, but also kind and generous. Some referred to their lifestyle as frontier survival. Litsa simply considered it as people having respect for human life in an often harsh and demanding environment.

The ranch was set in beautiful country, with green hills and meadows that would burst forth with every color of the rainbow come to earth in the spring. Wildlife was abundant, although sometimes threatening to the sheep. The air was fresh and the night sky glittered with millions of twinkling stars. It was home, her home, Gus' home. It would never be the same if he didn't return. She silently prayed again that he would recover completely to walk the grassy pastures with her and tell his captivating stories again in the light of a campfire.

The Sunday after Gus and been admitted to the hospital, the Sheep Growers' Association had called a meeting together to offer their assistance to Litsa and her mother while Gus was in rehabilitation. Many old and dear friends of the family, and some folks she didn't even know, were at the meeting. One man, in particular, who appeared to be in his late thirties, kept glancing over at her. She became aware of a strange sense of familiarity, yet was certain she didn't know him. He didn't seem to be a friend of anyone else at the meeting, as she never saw him talk with anyone who was there.

When the meeting had adjourned, everyone was invited to the ranch. It was as if Litsa had grown up on potluck dinners. For every occasion it was a reason to get together, but this time it was a special one. There was so much food on that table it seemed they were planning on feeding the entire county. Everyone had a favorite story to tell about Gus inducing tears as well as laughter. It was a gathering of love and Litsa and her mother were deeply grateful for the blessing of these caring country folks.

When the last of the visitors had finally departed, Litsa stood at the door watching them leave and thinking how wonderful it was to have such a foundation of friends for support in times of distress. Her mother, weary from the events of the day, had gone to bed leaving the table clearing to Litsa. The sun was setting in a vibrant sunset of color. She leaned against the doorway, deep in her thoughts, when suddenly she saw the man, who had kept glancing her way during the meeting, coming up the walk. She hadn't noticed him during the potluck, and now it was obvious he hadn't been there earlier with the rest of the people.

"Are you Litsa?" he asked as he came toward her.

Drawing back into the house she watched him warily. "Yes," she replied hesitantly. "Do I know you?"

"No, I'm afraid you don't," he said smiling. "My name is Jeff and I have been working with your grandfather for some time now. He wanted me to give you some papers he had kept for you. One is an old map. Mind if I come in?" he said looking past Litsa at the food still remaining visible on the table.

"Oh…Yes," Litsa said feeling rather off balance. Her mind reacted in a strange way as she looked into his face. "I'm sorry, I didn't mean to be rude. Please come in. Would you like something to eat?" she offered, gesturing toward the table where several dishes were still waiting to be emptied and put away. In her mind she was asking herself why she felt so weird.

"As a matter of fact I could use a bite," Jeff said smiling into her eyes. "It's been a long day and I just forgot to get dinner, I guess." His laughter was melodious and his eyes had a soft twinkle. He had a dimple on one side, which caused Litsa to smile involuntarily as it was a special feature she appreciated.

"There's plenty here so just help yourself," she said with a grin.

Jeff picked up a plate and piled it high with food. Litsa was thinking that maybe he hadn't eaten all day by the looks of that plate. He was dressed in typical western gear and had hung his cowboy hat on the rack when he came in. He had broad shoulders and narrow hips, a strong-looking body seemingly gained from working a ranch, a roughshod sort of appearance. He was a little less than six feet tall, dark brownish-black hair, and dark eyes that seemed to shimmer in the light of the dining room chandelier. He looked to Litsa like he could be part Indian, but definitely not of Greek lineage, with dark tanned skin and high cheekbones, and an ever so slight Roman nose. His hair was pulled back in a long ponytail that dropped several inches below his collar. Litsa couldn't help thinking how handsome he was, but also wondered how he fit in with her grandfather.

Jeff sat down to eat and, after several mouthfuls, finally looked up to see Litsa staring at him. "I'm so sorry," he said quietly. "This food just hits the spot. I was hungrier than I thought."

Litsa just laughed pleasantly and excused herself to take the empty dishes to the kitchen and let him finish his meal in solitude. She stayed out of sight for several minutes while he cleaned his plate. When she returned he was wiping his lips with a napkin and smiling his satisfaction. "That was some meal!" he said with obvious gratitude. "Thank you for feeding a starving cowboy."

Litsa nodded smiling. "Glad you enjoyed it.." She picked up his empty plate and tools and started toward the kitchen.

"Is there a place we can go and talk?" he asked as she crossed the room. "Maybe out on the porch?" He shot her a questioning look.

"Uh…sure," she replied over her shoulder as she entered the kitchen. "I'll be there in a couple of minutes." When Litsa returned to the dining room, he had already gone out the door and she heard his boots scraping the wooden porch floor and the creak of the old rocking chair as he sat down. She took a shawl off the hat rack by the door and stepped out into the cool night air.

Litsa wasn't alarmed to have this stranger come to the house and have a meal. Her home was a large sheep ranch and they often were looking for help to herd the sheep. Sometimes it was Indians or folks from Mexico who came by for a bite to eat and to inquire about work. Sometimes they would end up staying for as long as two years. Upon leaving to return to their families, still back in Mexico or on the reservation, they would then send a cousin or some other relative back to take their place.

"Your grandfather is a fine man," Jeff began as Litsa seated herself in the porch swing." He never harmed anyone and always had great respect for the land he traveled and lived in."

Litsa listened to this stranger's voice and was mesmerized by the gentleness it conveyed. She tried to watch him inconspicuously from the corner of her eye, wondering why he stirred an inexplicable sense of familiarity and trust in her.

"Did you work for Gus at the ranch here or in Utah?" she asked, trying to understand how he came to know Gus so well.

"I have known Gus for many years since my early days. I've worked in both Colorado and Utah with him. Did he ever tell you about the time he was in Dark Canyon in a very remote and primitive area, when some Indians tried to run him off?" he asked her. He was looking past her, into the night as he spoke, and his voice sounded very far away.

"Why, yes," she managed to say casually, trying to conceal her surprise. Gus said she was the only one he had ever told about that incident. Again she remembered Grandfather whispering in her ear at the hospital and how her spine tingled afterward whenever she thought about it.

"And Gus gave you something, didn't he? A small piece of gold?"

Litsa nodded and instinctively reached her hand into her pocket, then remembered where she had hidden the object Gus had given her.

"I have come to take you to the place where he encountered those people. I have a map here for you to study. You must not show this to anyone, not even your mother. Gus entrusted you with his sacred discovery and you must not reveal anything about it to anyone or you will never see that of which he spoke." Jeff's face was in the shadow, yet Litsa could see the gleam in his eyes and feel the stern tone of his voice as he spoke.

"I must go now. I will be back again in a few weeks to plan our trip to the canyons. Remember, you must tell no one where you are going or why you go there." With that, Jeff rose, stepped off the porch and trotted into the dark, disappearing moments after leaving the dim light from the house.

13

Litsa sat there a long time looking out into the dark and listening to the creaking of the porch swing. She was tired from the busy day and evening, and now she wasn't even sure what had just happened. Was it real or was she dreaming again? To the north she saw a falling star as it trailed it's dying light earthward. Then she rose and went into the house and to bed, and in her dream the star was Jeff going away into the night, into the darkness of the canyons, into a whirling night sky. And she saw Gus, in his younger form, smiling and handing her the gold piece. She heard the soft sound of a breeze blowing in the window, and she slept soundly until daylight.

Chapter 3

Sophia Pappas moved back to her father's ranch when Litsa was only two years old, after her husband had left her and Litsa without warning. Gus and his wife Marika graciously took them in and helped them begin a new life. Their son, Dino, had been killed only two years earlier when his horse reared and fell on him during a hunting trip up on the Grand Mesa near Grand Junction. Gus was deeply distraught, but when Sophia and Litsa came to the ranch to live, the gleam came back into his eyes and his laughter resounded again. Litsa became the light in his life and his reason to carry on.

Her grandparents loved and indulged Litsa, and she adored them. Marika became seriously ill when Litsa was seven years old and died of pneumonia shortly after Christmas that year. It was a sad and difficult time for them all, but the strength of the family prevailed and they held together drawing strength from one another. Gus had become the dominant man in Litsa's life and she cherished and respected him for all the years he had sheltered and provided for her and her mother.

Gus's parents had come to America from Greece following the turn of the century to escape the turmoil their country was going through. Gus's family and two uncles settled in Colorado and were doing quite well with sheep ranching. Gus was born in 1917 in Watson, Utah. As he got older, he became restless after leaving college, and went to Greece to live for a number of years learning the language and customs of his native country. He returned to the United States seeking work and decided to look for adventure in the West. Living a simple life with meager belongings, he worked various jobs, mostly with sheep ranches, trailing sheep in eastern Utah and the western slope of Colorado. There he gained enough knowledge and experience to undertake his own sheep ranching endeavor. When Gus and Marika married, Gus made a loan from his father-in-law to purchase land south of Grand Junction. He decided on two hundred acres in Colorado, in the Hubbard Creek area, the high country north of Paonia.

Gus knew how other sheep ranches operated in that area, moving their flocks down to lower pasture in Utah during the winter so they could lamb and be sheared early in the spring. He then followed suit and bought two hundred fifty acres of land in Utah. With outfits in both areas, he could herd the sheep to the high country of Colorado during the summers and back down into Utah for winter pasturing, sending the lambs to market in September the way the other ranchers did.

Gus was successful with his ranching and over the years had traveled much of the land of eastern Utah and western Colorado. He was always enchanted by its spacious vistas and rugged terrain. Canyons abound in Utah, especially in an area known as Canyon Lands. There, many secret places are hidden from view among the eroded sandstone cliffs cut by runoff streams from the higher elevations and the Colorado and San Juan Rivers.

Trailing sheep for days on end permitted much time for thinking. Gus contemplated the land he traversed and the people who had inhabited it many centuries before his presence. Some say the area is still inhabited by spirits of the ancient pueblo dwellers, the Anasazi, who hunted, grew corn, and sang their ceremonial songs among the canyons. Gus had heard their songs in the wind, in the rhythm of rain on the sandstone ridges, in the seasonal streams that cut their paths through the hills and valleys. But he also said he had heard them singing and chanting somewhere in the canyons late in the evening after the sun had set and he sat alone at a glowing campfire in the silence of the canyon world.

Frequently his excursions had resulted in discoveries of archeological and anthropological value. The Anasazi had left considerable evidence throughout the area surrounding the four corners of Utah, Arizona, New Mexico and Colorado that revealed details of their lives. To this day one can see pottery shards, arrowheads, picture stories and especially, the impressive structures they built of rock and clay. One of the more interesting and intriguing finds were the petroglyphs, which could be found throughout the area of western Utah and eastern Colorado. They are particularly numerous in the Sego Canyon area north of Crescent Junction, Utah, where Gus kept his flock in the winters.

He wondered about what stories the strange picture writings were meant to convey, as they were difficult to decipher, even for the experts. Curiously, one question remains unanswered, even by the ancient writing. What happened to these industrious aboriginal people? Some say the Anasazi simply disappeared, but it seems more reasonable to believe they just moved and merged, integrating themselves among other Southwestern tribes, mainly the Hopi and Zuni, in a continual struggle for survival against the cycles of nature, and possibly other peoples of the area.

Gus wasn't a greedy hunter of artifacts. His interest was far deeper than that of monetary value. He cherished the items he came across and only kept a select few to identify the places he found them and the people he yearned to understand. He wrote in a journal about his finds, and kept it concealed from anyone other than Litsa. He told her how he always offered a sort of prayer to the spirits of the ancient people who had left the artifacts behind, asking their permission to keep an item for his private collection.

Gus knew that due to their developed building skill, the Anasazi were considered to be puebloan Indians because they constructed their villages out of stone and clay. Pueblo, in Spanish, means village, and the Spanish were the first foreigners known to encounter the Indian tribes of the Southwest and see their pueblos. Oftentimes the Anasazi would build in a shallow cave-like indention in a cliff high in the walls of a canyon, where they used ladders to go in and out of the pueblo. This offered protection from enemies and most wild animals. The largest settlements of puebloan people currently are in New Mexico along the Rio Grande River, where they continue to inhabit their villages to this day. Others are in western New Mexico at Acoma, and on the Hopi reservation in northern Arizona.

Gus had talked to many people who lived and traveled the same country as he, trailing sheep or herding cattle, and had learned much about the Anasazi. He made trips to the pueblos at Hovenweep, Mesa Verde and other sites in the Four Corners area to study the remarkable structures they had built and deserted. He had been told by a few who were well versed in the history of these people that they had lived in the Southwest since before the birth of Christ.

Chapter 4

At their campfires or in front of a cozy fire at the ranch, Gus would sit for hours telling Litsa stories of the tribe that had seemingly vanished nearly a thousand years ago, and how they had built villages in the cliffs and canyons all over the Southwest. Sometimes, at play, she would pretend she was an Anasazi woman and try grinding corn on a rock until her hands were raw and sore, or attempt to make a crude pot out of the chalky Utah clay. Grandfather would nod and smile approvingly at her childish imitation and, as she grew older, she also became interested in the history of the Anasazi. She embraced a deep sense of a strong connection with the people she never quite understood.

Litsa loved to hear the stories Gus would tell about being in the Utah canyon lands and spending nights in caves. There he found ancient drawings on the walls and pieces of pottery scattered on the floors. He would closely examine these relics making certain they were always returned to their original positions. There were also stories of cowboys and how they would leave firewood in the cave for the next cowboy that needed to stay the night. It would be placed in a neat pile according to the cowboy rule. Litsa loved the thought that the early adventurers and cowboys respected the land and the history, and that they held each other in respect as well.

Before deciding on a career in nursing, Litsa had studied archaeology and paleontology at Northern Arizona College in Flagstaff. During her third year, she made a trip to Greece to visit some of the historical sites of her great-grandfather's birthplace. She found it to be an intriguing land for exploring and learning, but the call to nursing was more practical it seemed, and so she returned to school at the University of Arizona in Tucson to accomplish that goal and receive her nursing degree.

One particular story Gus had told Litsa about his travels in Utah always made her spine tingle with excitement as she imagined what had taken place. It was in the Canyon Lands called Dark Canyon, a primitive area southwest of Moab, Utah in a maze of sandstone canyons with steep narrow walls. As he was heading back toward camp late in the afternoon he had seen a flash of something in a remote area of the canyon he was riding above on the mesa. His curiosity goading him, he turned his horse down a precipitous old trail toward the direction of whatever he had seen. Winding down the trail he realized it was not an animal trail, but seemed to be a very old footpath with stone markers at intervals. When he reached the canyon floor the path looked as if it had been deliberately erased in places to make it less visible. As he came around a blind bend in the canyon trail his horse suddenly balked and nearly reared back on him. Out of the rocky shadows leapt a half dozen Indians yelling and startling his horse so that it turned and bolted back up the trail in the direction he had come.

Their appearance was extraordinary, not that of the Ute, Paiute, Navajo or even Apache, but clearly different from any of those. They wore breechclouts and simple headbands with an unfamiliar feather of bright color

20

in them. The designs on their arms were unlike any Gus had seen in the native regions he had explored, but they reminded him of the petroglyphs he had seen. The Indians had waved their arms and shouted in their native tongue in an obvious attempt to run him off and, as he quickly departed, he made mental notes as to the location for future reference.

When Gus would tell his stories, Litsa would listen intently, trying to picture herself wherever the story took them, often falling asleep in his arms and dreaming about what he had told her as she snuggled in her bed. He often told her the story about a lost city somewhere in the canyons. She loved the country she had grown up in, and hoped one day to be able to explore the land and canyons of her grandfather's tales, perhaps to make her own unique adventures and discoveries. Maybe she, too, would hear the ancient people sing and chant their ceremonial songs somewhere in the mysterious labyrinth of canyons. Maybe even one day she would find the lost city.

Gus was doing well following his surgery and was recovering nicely at the rehabilitation center. Litsa never mentioned the gold nugget or the map again since she wanted to keep him from having any more stress. It seemed like he didn't want to talk about it either, as he hadn't brought the subjects up. He had simply told her she would understand it all very soon.

Litsa had studied the map from every angle, and there seemed to be nothing there out of the ordinary, she thought, other than it was a very old map. It looked like many canyons running off in every direction, many of them coming to a dead end. She laid it down on the table next to the gold piece Gus had given her at the hospital knowing there was some kind of a connection between the two, but what? The secret Gus had whispered in her ear didn't make much sense and her imagination was weary trying to conceive every possibility. She hadn't seen or heard anything from Jeff either, so she was having a tough time understanding what the nugget and the map were really all about. All she could do was wait and see if Jeff would return.

Three weeks after Gus was placed in rehabilitation, Litsa flew back to Tucson to pack her belongings and head home for the summer. As she drove back up to Colorado she contemplated the job opportunities she had seen at the employment center, wondering where she should go to begin her career. There were a number of options in the Western states, and that was her first choice of areas. Her plan was to send out applications during the summer so she could start work in the fall. She also thought about what had taken place when grandfather was in the hospital, and all he had told her, wondering if he would give her further information when she returned to the ranch. The secret they shared perplexed her, especially when she thought about Jeff and how he might be involved.

The days were getting warmer as summer drifted gently into the high country and Litsa had been helping with the late lambs and ewes that were ready to be trucked to the high country. It had been weeks since grandfather's heart attack and he was doing remarkably well. She had all but forgotten about Jeff, the map and the gold nugget, when from the corner of her eye she saw him standing at the corner of the loading chute watching her.

"Damn you scare me!" she exclaimed turning toward him. "Why are you watching me that way, and why are you back here?" She continued working with the sheep for a few more minutes. Jeff could see she was having trouble getting them to go up the ramp to the waiting trucks. She walked over to him calming her frustration and feeling regretful about her initial reaction.

"I'm sorry, Jeff. I didn't mean to be rude," she said brushing her pants, and shirtsleeves to get some of the dust off. "I guess I look a bit of a mess. It's been a long, dusty day and these lambs and ewes don't exactly want to take a ride to the high country," she frowned.

Jeff smiled, walked over to the gate, opened it, and in no time flat all the ewes and lambs ran right up the ramp and into the trailer. "How did you do that?" Litsa said in total surprise. "I've never seen sheep do that before! Tell me what you did."

"It's an old secret my people taught me many years ago," Jeff said with a grin.

"Well, I would sure love to learn that one. Sometimes these sheep are not very smart," Litsa said turning toward the house. "Would you like something to drink?" she asked.

"Actually, I came to see if you were ready to go to Dark Canyon," Jeff told her. Gus said if anything ever happened to him I was to show you the way. I stopped by to see him yesterday. He's doing very well, isn't he?"

Litsa just stood there staring at Jeff. "Did you hear me?" he said.

"Yes, I was just wondering why my grandfather sent you to take me to the canyon lands."

As he followed her to the house he said, "You'll see when we get to the Dark Canyon. It's a very dangerous place for a young lady like you to go alone, and since I already know the area, well, I guess you know the rest…and time is running out," he said gently but with conviction. Litsa thought he was talking about time running out and summer would soon be over. None too soon for her as it had been a very warm spring and summer. Autumn would be a pleasant change.

Litsa looked at him with eyes leveled and said, "Okay...but when did you want to go?" She could feel her curiosity building, but the eerie feeling was with her too, and she remained cautious. Besides, she thought it would

23

be a welcome change to get away. The sheep would be up in the high country with the herders and Gus was much improved. She was looking forward to spending some time in the canyon lands.

"In five days. If you go over to Moab you can take highway 191 south turning off onto highway 211 at Church Rock, and meet me at Newspaper Rock. Do you know where that is?" he said as she handed him a glass of lemonade.

"Yes, I've been by there," Litsa nodded, "but never actually been to Newspaper Rock. Gus talked about it many times."

"From there we will have to ride horseback," Jeff told her. Gus said you were an experienced rider and that I won't have to worry about you keeping up. Litsa blushed and looked away. "Yes, Gus was a good teacher. Do you need a horse?" Litsa asked him.

"Yes, if you have a good one that can handle tough trails," he smiled looking toward the corral.

"I have two of the best horses there are. They've been on many trails in Utah and are well behaved. You can turn them loose and they'll stay right in the area without putting hobbles on them." she told him proudly.

One was Gus's horse, Starlight, who had been all over eastern Utah, as well as in Arizona, Colorado and New Mexico. The other was Litsa's horse, Favorito. She led Jeff to the edge of the pasture beyond the corral, pointing to the horses she had mentioned. "They are endurance horses with manners. The best!"

"We'll need a pack mule, too," he said looking across at the mule in the pasture.

"That would be Benny," she laughed. "He's one of the best pack mules we've ever had." Litsa had been riding since she was very young. In her late teens she would frequently take her horse out and go camping alone or with her grandfather. Her mother always said Litsa could handle a horse and gun better than any man she ever met. Litsa believed that, too.

"Okay, so I'll meet you at Newspaper Rock this coming Friday. I should be there early in the afternoon. Be prepared for an unusual adventure. And remember, no one needs to know exactly where you are going," he reminded her. "Just say you will be in the canyon lands in eastern Utah."

"And what if something bad happens?" she queried with raised eyebrows.

"Just trust that you'll be okay while you're with me. Gus will know about this trip. He's the only one who will know exactly where we are going," he told her. Then, in moments, he was gone.

Litsa stood holding the two empty lemonade glasses and feeling strange again. It was as if he threw her off balance somehow. But he said her grandfather would know where they were going, so she shrugged her shoulders and went into the house wondering about where, exactly, they *were* going.

On the trip to Hubbard Creek later that afternoon, Litsa recalled some of Gus's stories of how the cowboys would hide out in the canyons. She recalled his story of Butch Cassidy and the Sundance Kid who, after robbing a bank, would return to the canyon lands to their hideout and wait till things calmed down. They knew the sheriff would never follow them into the canyon lands. Gus's stories were always fun for Litsa to hear and she would ask for them to be told time and time again.

For the next five days Litsa had much to do at the ranch getting the horses ready for the trip. She had to get them shod and make sure they were in good shape for rigorous travel. Instinctively, she followed the rules Gus had given her years ago about preparing for a horseback trip. It was critical to make sure everything was done with care and concern, making sure to pack the first aid kit, and a slicker. Sometimes a summer storm could come up fast. She had seen that happen many times when she was in the high country while helping Gus with the sheep. There were times the lightening would frighten the flocks and scatter them, and it would take two days to round all of them up. Usually a few would be missing, taken by either a cougar or coyotes.

The five days went by fast and Litsa was getting more excited by the day. She was always game to try something new and, since Gus had told her so much about Dark Canyon, she could hardly wait to explore it herself. Then having Jeff as her guide made it that much more exciting. There was something about him that made her feel very different in a most unusual way.

Sophia asked her where she was going with two horses and a pack mule. "Oh, mother, it's the chance of a lifetime," Litsa told her. "I'm going to find the lost city Grandfather told me so much about."

"By yourself?" her mother asked with a look of concern.

"Please, don't worry mother. I'll be fine," she smiled. She wasn't sure about how to explain Jeff being on the trip, so she just didn't mention him at all. Sophia never questioned her about why she was taking Gus's horse with her. Litsa would have to lie to Sophia, and that was one thing she wouldn't want to do. Sophia probably would get an answer that she didn't understand any way.

"Yes, I'm sure you will be," Sophia laughed. "Your grandfather made a boy out of you!"

With that Litsa laughed. "Oh, mother, try not to worry," she said giving her mother a hug. She hurried out then, leaving her mother standing at the door. As Sophia stood there gazing after her daughter, the reality of any unique situation, when confronted by it, would always make her shake her head and mumble in Greek, "Tiv ekar'e avdpas" (he made a man out of you).

Chapter 5

     Friday morning Litsa loaded the horses and Benny, the mule, with food, map, nugget, sleeping bag, clothes and the first aid kit. She left a trail of dust behind her as she drove out of the driveway, singing to the radio as loud as she could. This was something she had wanted to do all her life and now she was finally getting the chance. A tear came to her eye as she thought how much she would miss Gus not being there with her. She had told him about Jeff coming to the house, and the plans they had made. He didn't say much, but relaxed in his chair at the rehab center and smiled, knowing that Litsa was going on the trip of her dreams. She knew he was getting better and she would have a wonderful story to tell him when she got back.

     It was about noon when she pulled into Moab to fill the truck up with gas and grab a bite to eat. She checked the horses and Benny, to make sure they were enduring the trip well. Getting back on the highway she began thinking about the things Gus had told her about the country she was going to ride and camp in. She remembered him telling about Newspaper Rock and the nice campgrounds that had been put in, where there were trails you could hike or do some trail riding. That's where she should meet Jeff. She hoped that he was going to be there, that it wasn't just talk.

There was hardly any traffic as she drove south on highway 191 so she relaxed and enjoyed the drive. The sun was bright in the cloudless sky and everything seemed to stand out distinctly as she traveled. She turned west on highway 211 about a half hour out of Moab. The road was well paved and, after about 15 miles, it dropped down into a beautiful canyon with large cottonwood trees. There was a small stream running along the road and on the other side were high cliffs. She saw the sign that read, Newspaper Rock, 500 Feet.

Driving slowly she could see all the things Gus had mentioned, even the strange looking rock formations he'd told her about so many times. She came upon another sign with an arrow pointing toward the parking area. About fifty feet down the road she saw Jeff silhouetted against the afternoon sun. Upon seeing him again, she felt that same mixture of thrill and excitement edged with apprehension that she experienced whenever he was around.

"Boy, I am sure glad to see you! This is so far out here," she said as she got out of the truck. "How did you get here with no truck or horse?" she asked, looking around for some sign of how he traveled. He didn't answer her, but smiled and moved to the back of the horse trailer and opened the door.

Benny and Favorito backed right out, but Starlight snorted and flared his nostrils. Jeff held his hand up and made a slight movement with it while looking Starlight directly in the eye. Then he reached up and touched his forehead. Litsa had never seen Starlight act up like that, but in just moments he had settled down and dropped his head almost to the ground. Jeff gave him a rub on the neck and said something in a strange language, one she had never heard before.

"We need to saddle the horses and move out before it gets too late," Jeff told her as he led the horses to the spring to get a drink of water. "We can camp at Elk Ridge tonight. There is plenty of food and water there for the animals."

He began saddling the horses while she locked up the truck and trailer. She took care to see that all she had brought along was safely packed on Benny. In less than a half hour they were mounted and on their way across the small stream heading toward the trail. A small sign with an arrow pointing to the west said, Canyonland Trail.

She watched Jeff as he rode in front of her on Starlight, the jet-black quarter horse Gus had ridden for years. He was eighteen years old, but didn't look it at all. They acted as if they had been riding together before. Every movement was as if they had joined spirits.

Who was this man, Jeff? She pictured him as maybe a chief or a member of high rank, or councilman, in an Indian tribe. Whatever he was, he was very capable on horseback. Litsa would be keeping her eyes on him, for sure.

During the ride neither of them spoke much. Litsa was enjoying the scenery, the plants and rocks, and had time to study them in passing. She was riding Favorito, a big bay horse with strong Morgan and quarter mix. She had raised him from a colt and they had always been partial to one another. Favorito seemed instinctively to take care of his mistress. He was always alert with his ears forward, and watching for any signs of danger. The trail quickly became steep with loose gravel, but Benny had no trouble getting a good foothold. He was a seasoned mule and had been on more trips than Litsa could count.

When they topped out on the mesa, the view was wonderful, and Litsa was exhilarated with the expanse of canyons she could see. Jeff turned and grinned at her expressive face as she gazed across the land in admiration for the beauty and spaciousness.

"Looks like another world, doesn't it?" he said over his shoulder.

"It's incredible!" she replied edging Favorito up closer to Starlight. "I haven't seen it from this point before. It simply takes my breath away."

They had been riding for about four hours when they approached Elk Ridge. Litsa was glad they had arrived, as she was getting hungry and she knew Jeff probably would appreciate a good meal. They stopped under a tall pine tree and Jeff dismounted then went around to help Litsa down. She leaned over and he reached up and put his hands firmly on her waist. Slowly he let her slide down the front of him, looking deep into her eyes. Litsa felt the man in him, and it sent a bold chill right through her. She blushed as he let her go with a sly grin. Dropping her head and looking down, she felt flushed and was trying to find the right words to say.

"I'll get the horses tied for the night," Jeff said as he moved away and led them toward an open area. Litsa stood there for a few moments trying to soak in what had just happened. Her whole body felt weak, but she wasn't sure if it was from riding Favorito or from the sensation of Jeff helping her down from the saddle.

"I'll get the food from Benny's pack and start a fire," she said trying to bring herself out of the stupor. "I brought some stew mother made, will that be okay?" she asked taking the pack off Benny.

"Yes, anything sounds good," Jeff said as he tended the horses.

After they had eaten and cleaned up, Jeff spread his saddle blanket out on the ground and put the saddle down for a pillow, leaving Litsa to fend for herself. She got her saddle blanket and spread it out on the other side of the fire. They spoke briefly about the canyons and she told him what Gus had told her about the area. Jeff nodded and said he, too, had been in the canyonland country many times giving brief descriptions of places he knew. Then he said goodnight and lay down to sleep. With that, Litsa laid back and looked at the treetops and stars beyond. It had been quite a day, she thought. Wondering about Jeff and how far they were going, she quickly fell asleep.

The sunlight was just beginning to come to the ridge when Litsa opened her eyes to see Jeff sitting on a rock nearby, staring at her. "Why didn't you wake me?" she asked sitting up.

"You looked so peaceful I didn't want to disturb you," he said smiling.

"I'm sorry. I'll get some breakfast and coffee on," and with that she jumped up and almost fell over the saddle. She could feel her whole body blush.

Jeff only grinned and said, "Let me help."

He started a fire almost instantly, as if by magic, and had the coffee heating by the time she got the eggs and bacon out of the packs. She only shook her head in disbelief. She knew she was overwhelmed by his abilities and the mystique of his personality, but she didn't know how to approach questioning him. So she accepted things as they happened, strange as they may be, hoping they would explain themselves out before too long.

The sun was bright in the morning sky by the time they mounted their horses. They began heading southwest toward Dark Canyon. The quiet beauty of the hills and the hypnotic oneness with her horse was pure joy to Litsa as she rode. Thoughts of her grandfather riding this country, trailing sheep with his border collie, Yu, surrounded her with a sense of warmth. She imagined the two of them alone on the ridges, Gus whistling long and hard and Yu scrambling to keep the ewes and lambs heading in the right direction. She

33

understood, finally, the magic and the mystical qualities he had experienced years ago. This was what Gus wanted her to know, and what he wanted her to feel.

They rode from the hills across mesas and into small canyons, which changed in appearance as they went from one into the next. At midday they finally stopped to eat lunch under some old ironwood trees. After letting the horses rest and graze for a short time, they were back on the trail. The day was very warm and the trail was dry and dusty. It looked like there had been no rain for months.

Litsa knew, from her studies of archeology, that thousands of years had made parts of southeastern Utah, Colorado, Arizona and New Mexico a somewhat desolate land. The years without much rain had created a drought-damaged environment there. Most of the areas had been set aside as park lands or Indian reservations, and fire warnings were prevalent between rains.

Chapter 6

The Cottonwood River made its way south to meet with the San Juan River, then on to the Colorado River, then to Glen Canyon. For thousands of years these rivers had washed away the earth to make great canyons, the deepest one being the Grand Canyon. Litsa had been there several times, making the trek down to the bottom. She never got tired of the beauty of that canyon. She thought about it as she rode along, and her other favorite canyons at Mesa Verde and Canyon De Chelly. She could only imagine how the Indians had lived in those places many years ago, and what had happened to them.

Suddenly a shot rang out making Favorito lurch off the trail. "What was that?!" Litsa asked as she eased him back onto the trail. In one swift movement Jeff was off Starlight and on the ground. He reached down and grabbed a four-foot long rattlesnake, cut its head off, then took the rattles off. The snake was still moving, trying to coil around Jeff's arm. He looked at Litsa with a victorious grin.

"Guess what's for dinner tonight?"

Litsa had heard rattlesnake was a delight, but never had the courage to try it. Tonight she would have that chance, she thought uncertainly.

The sun was behind clouds as the evening drew nigh, making it seem darker than usual. As they came into a narrow place in a canyon, Jeff turned to Litsa and said, "I think we will make nightfall here."

Litsa pulled Favorito to a stop and jumped off. She didn't want to be embarrassed again with Jeff helping her off the horse. She got a butterfly feeling though, when she thought about it. While she tied the horses and was taking Benny's packs off, Jeff had already started a fire and the heat felt good as the desert air was cooling down. The clouds were building off to the west making it dark early and cooler than usual.

" Looks like it might rain tonight," Jeff said as he began preparing dinner. "Be sure to get your slicker out." He went about fixing the snake after very carefully removing the skin, then putting a stick through it to let it roast above the fire. He turned it slowly while Litsa heated some beans from the ranch garden she had brought along. It was a most delightful meal. Jeff looked at her grinning, and with a wink said, "How do you like the snake?"

"Not bad," Litsa said. "It tastes almost like chicken, but I think I prefer the chicken."

They had just finished eating when the first raindrop fell, then a flash of lightning and thunder so loud it startled the horses. "It's a good thing they were tired tonight," Litsa said as she scanned the area around them. She saw a small space where she could crawl up under a rock for protection from the rain. Grabbing her slicker, she was gone in a moment.

Jeff didn't even bother putting the fire out. He, too, ran for cover. It was well into the evening when the storm started to let up. The thunder had been so loud one couldn't even hear what the other was saying. It was dark and chilly when the rain finally stopped. Litsa was happy about the rain, after thinking all day how dry it was. Everything smelled so fresh and clean.

The first couple of days Litsa spent most of the time studying the land around her trying to recall familiarities from all her grandfather had told her. While she focused on rocks and plants and the different colors in the canyons, Jeff tended to the trail, as he seemed to know where he was going. From time to time she would see petroglyphs on rocks and she wondered if that was how he knew the trail, or if he did it from memory.

Each day she was more intrigued watching him. He was definitely a mystery, but she enjoyed his company and they got along well. He didn't act like an Indian, or at least the ones she knew. There was something different about him. He made every effort to show Litsa many unusual sites along the way as they rode, sometimes telling little stories about them.

When he talked, often it was about personal things. He told her a little about when he was a small boy and his family was continually on the move to keep away from the enemy. One strange thing he said that got Litsa's attention was how they had moved from canyon to canyon as they were trying to find safety. Litsa wasn't sure what to make of what he was saying, but she listened to every word he said, although a bit puzzled. The way he was talking it was as though he was telling about things in the past, far back in the past.

It rained again that night after they had bedded down, but they had found a shallow cave, which protected them. Litsa awoke in the middle of the night. The campfire was just about out and she looked to see if Jeff was asleep. Surprised to see he was nowhere around, she got up and went out of the cave. When she looked to the east she saw him standing on a rock outcrop above camp, holding his hands up to the stars and chanting softly. The sky had cleared and she noticed the stars were exceptionally bright, and one star stood out brighter than the rest. She thought maybe he was talking to his ancestors in an ancient language.

She went back into the cave thinking he was truly a mystery. She wondered if maybe he had eaten some Mescaline, a visual drug named after the Mescalero Apaches, made from the Divine cactus, which grows in the southwest and Mexico. She had seen some earlier that morning on the trail and knew under a controlled situation that it would wear off in about ten hours. Jeff, however, seemed like he had everything under control. Litsa knew from her chemistry studies that mescaline was about four thousand times less potent than peyote, which also comes from a cactus. Having considered all that and being too tired to fret, she lay down and went back to sleep.

The next morning she asked Jeff about what she had seen. He didn't say much, just told her he was having trouble sleeping. After a quick breakfast he got the horses and Benny ready for the day's ride. He said they should be at the Cottonwood River by evening. "We'll make camp there tonight," he told her.

The terrain in the canyon lands was constantly changing, and now it was becoming more like mountain riding. This was great for Litsa as she had done a lot of trail riding and knew Favorito and Starlight were strong horses. They could be trusted and they were used to mountain trails, so the Manti-La Sal forest was of little concern to her.

The rain the night before had made the ground slippery and the horses were having difficulty getting good footing. Benny had no trouble at all as this was his favorite. Being a mule, he was sure footed and seemed to actually enjoy walking in the mud. They followed a narrow trail most of the way and every so often a deer would jump out and run in front of them. Little squirrels would chatter at them from the trees and chipmunks would chase each other in what seemed like play. It was all a welcoming site to these strangers to the forest. Litsa loved the wildlife and there was so much to learn just by watching.

When they stopped for lunch, Jeff spread a blanket on the ground in some shade and Litsa got the biscuits and dried beef from Benny's pack. After they ate, Litsa laid back on the blanket closing her eyes and enjoying the warm sun.

She was awakened by a shake on the shoulder. Startled, she sat up quickly. Jeff was standing over her with his head slightly tilted, and a gentle look in his eyes. "You fell asleep."

"For how long? What time is it?" Litsa asked pushing her hair back out of her face.

"You slept about an hour. Don't worry, we have time and you needed the rest," Jeff said offering his hand to Litsa. As she got up she fell right into his arms. He held her tight, looking deeply into her eyes, then in a flash their lips met. It felt like a bolt of lightning had shot through her veins, taking her breath away. Of all the men she had dated she'd never had a passionate kiss like that. It was a kiss that lasted for a few minutes. Litsa returned the kiss and it felt as if she was melting right into his arms. She didn't want to fight the feeling or have it end, ever.

Jeff took her by the shoulders and gently pushed her back. "I'm sorry. I had no right to do that," he said looking bewildered and sad. Litsa blushed, putting her hand to her lips, but not wanting to wipe the kiss away. He turned and walked over to the horses to tighten the cinches and check Benny's packs, then once again they were ready to go.

Litsa was in a quandary. What did this man want? Who is he, and better yet, what is he? She felt such affection toward him, but the mystical side of him warned her to be very careful. She knew there was much she didn't understand, so she sent her thoughts away and tried to simply enjoy the beauty of the land around them and the journey together. They didn't talk much that afternoon, but Litsa kept going over what had happened earlier, trying to calm her heart.

It was about seven in the evening when they came over the ridge where the trail led down to the river. Litsa could hear the river before it came into view and it was a welcome site, more beautiful than she could have imagined. As they were approaching the river two eagles flew over them seeming to wonder if these newcomers were a danger to the young they had in a nest at the top of a pine tree. They were screaming as they flew over, but Jeff held up his hand and said something in the strange language he spoke. The eagles circled around again, then took off to finish their hunting.

Litsa was amazed, and she couldn't help but wonder if he was a medicine man or some kind of brave warrior. He seemed to have some mystical power to command the animals and birds. She had studied the shamans and medicine men of many tribes and knew they had great knowledge of herbs, plants, animals, and the stars. Medicine men were healers and honored, trusted members of the tribe. But was he a shaman? And what tribe was he from? She hoped she would soon have answers to her questions.

Jeff was very familiar with the canyon lands and knew about all the animals and birds that are found there. Often he spoke to them in a language that was not that of the Navajo, Apache, or Ute, although there were a few words Litsa thought sounded like Hopi. She didn't know the Hopi language or customs as well as she knew those of the other tribes in that area. It was more of an ancient sound, like when he was chanting. She did hear him say, "We shall not disappear from this land, we and the land are one," but she wasn't sure how she knew what he had said. He was undoubtedly peculiar and unexplainable to her.

When they dismounted Litsa couldn't wait to get to the river. Three days on the trail and she was thrilled to get the chance to take a bath. While Jeff was tying the horses and making the fire, she went to the river and it was wonderfully cool and refreshing. The sky was still light and she remembered she had packed a folding fishing pole. With clean clothes and a renewed feeling, she got the pole out of the pack and went fishing. She had just flipped the line into the water when a nearly three-pound brown trout hit it and almost broke the pole.

Litsa was as determined to catch the fish as it was to get away. After nearly ten minutes she landed the fish. Jeff heard her scream with delight and had to go see what she was doing. She looked at him with a big grin and said, "You got dinner the other night…the snake. Tonight it's my turn to bring dinner to the fire." It was a good dinner, too, and she was quite proud of it. Even Jeff had to agree it was delicious.

After they had eaten all they could and put their blankets and saddles in place for the night, Jeff said," Litsa, I need to talk to you about where we are going. I know several years ago your grandfather rode into one of the canyons one day and some braves tried to run him off."

"Do you know why?" Litsa asked.

"Yes, you see it's a sacred place where long ago the people who lived in these canyons performed rituals. They believed the holes in the ground were where their spirits came into these canyons after they were born. It was the Shaman's job to fight for the good spirits. He could fly above to the spirit world or descend into the underworld, being stripped to a skeleton to be reassembled and reborn. His life was given to fighting evil spirits and

41

sorcerers and protecting the people from disease and famine. In the strictest sense, he was one who could will his spirit to leave the body and journey to the upper or lower worlds to serve his purpose."

"Why are you telling me all this?" Lisa said, even more puzzled than before.

"As we get closer to Dark Canyon you will notice strange things beginning to take place. I will be here by you to protect you from any harm. Do not be alarmed by what you see or think you see. There is a reason I'm telling you this now. Tomorrow we will be entering the Dark Canyon, and the deeper we get into the canyon the more you will have to trust me. Do you understand?" he asked her with determination in his voice.

"I think so," Litsa said hesitantly.

"Go now and get a good night's rest," he said with a tender smile.

Chapter 7

Very early in the morning Litsa awoke smelling the campfire. The sun was just peeking over the far edge of the horizon and Jeff was beginning to make breakfast. "Did you sleep well?" he asked her.

"Yes, well, sort of. Only I was thinking of what you said last night and it kept waking me up," Litsa answered.

"I just wanted to prepare you for what was coming," Jeff said with a look of concern in his eyes. "There are things you will need to know as we get deeper into the canyon."

Litsa helped saddle the horses and get Benny ready. "Today we will ride as far as we can into the canyon, then we will have to leave the horses and just take Benny with us," Jeff told her as he climbed into the saddle. "The trail will get too rough and steep for horses."

"They should be fine wherever we leave them if there's grass," Litsa told him. "They will stay around till we come back out of the canyon."

At first the trail was easy going, and then about an hour into the canyon the trail began to get narrow. Litsa heard something that sounded like bugs buzzing around her head but she couldn't see any. She thought how strange it was, like a tape recorder on fast track sounding like chipmunks.

She had to grin at her thought, remembering how she and her cousins, when they were very young, would tape a recording then play it fast. They would laugh at how funny it sounded.

Starlight and Favorito were having trouble getting good footing in the loose rock and were sliding on the trail. Jeff said he thought they needed to dismount and lead the horses to avoid the risk of having them fall. They led the horses a mile or so further where they came to a wide spot with a small creek running through it and plenty of grass. "This is where we will have to leave the horses," he said as he dismounted.

Happy to be rid of their saddles, the horses immediately laid down to roll, jumping up to shake. Having done that, they went right to eating.

"We will put the saddles and gear in that small cave," Jeff said pointing toward where a large creosote bush hid the opening. "They will be out of the weather there and safe until you return."

Back on the trail they wound around, crossing over dry creek beds and going further into a large canyon, which looked rugged and more winding than any Litsa had ever seen. As they hiked deeper into the canyon she was intoxicated by the beauty of the high cliffs and peacefulness of its depth. But it was also an eerie place and she was glad Jeff was there with her.

Around noon they stopped to eat and rest. Jeff had a concerned look on his face. "Litsa," he said, "I need to remind you not to be afraid of what you will see or hear. There will be strange things that you have never seen before. You will be perfectly safe as long as I am with you."

Again, Litsa was trying to figure out what he was talking about. Surely he knew the way into the hidden city. Was he trying to frighten her? Was the trust she had felt for him a mask to cover her excitement of wanting to learn more of the mystery of the lost city? Confused thoughts coupled with inexplicable fear kept her mind going in circles.

Jeff was acting more unusual as the day wore on. They had been hiking for about two hours when they came around a bend and into a dead-end cul-de-sac. He stopped suddenly. Litsa could hear faint sounds, which sounded like the same chanting she had heard Jeff make. He in return started to chant. Then he stepped up onto a large flat rock and held his hands up.

Litsa couldn't believe what she was seeing. Jeff was starting to disappear, fading in and out. She stood there in shock, but remembering what he had told her. She knew she had to keep her senses about her and stay calm. She had heard stories about a phenomenon called Spontaneous Involuntary Invisibility.   Did Jeff know the secret of how it was done? She stood there paralyzed for what seemed like forever, unable to take her eyes away from the rock he had been standing on. He was gone.

In a matter of not more than five minutes he began to reappear, but instead of being dressed in the old western clothes he had been wearing, he was the most beautiful figure Litsa had ever seen. He had a headdress on, with a gold strap over one shoulder, a gold band around his upper arm, a loincloth around his hips, and moccasins beaded in silver and gold on his feet. His hair was down blowing in the breeze. She could only stand and stare in amazement. As he came down off the rock he looked to her like pictures she had seen of Indian chieftains. Could he be an Anasazi Chief, she wondered in her dazed state of mind?

"Litsa", I'm sorry to frighten you like that," he told her smiling. "My name is not really Jeff, its Madia, which means 'one that dances with the stars.' I'm from the Anastasia band that came to live here almost a thousand years ago. My people were forced to stay in this canyon and we had to go

45

underground to survive. You heard a strange buzzing in your ears when we entered the canyon, didn't you?"

"Yes," Litsa said with a bewildered look on her face.

"That was my people's spirits welcoming you into their canyon. You see, after a thousand years all the spirits and myself desire to be free from this earth, and that is why you are here, to help us. Remember the gold nugget your grandfather Gus gave you at the hospital?" he asked her.

"Yes," Litsa nodded.

"That is the key you need to replace in order to free our spirits forever in time and space. You are the one chosen by the elders and I was sent to bring you here. You see…when your grandfather was run off that day by the warriors at the bend in the canyon, it was not done to frighten him. My people placed the gold nugget and old map near the trail where we knew he would return and surely find them."

"We have known for many years he would come this way that day, and we all waited patiently for him. We also knew he would one day tell you the secret and what the gold piece was for. We knew you were the one who would get the key. My people knew Gus could be trusted and would pass the secret on to you so that you could complete the circle. I went to work for him sometime ago so that I could gain his trust, and to locate you. He knew all about me, and that's why he wanted you to have the map and gold piece he found all those years ago on the trail. In the hospital he told you a secret when he gave you the nugget, didn't he?"

"Yes," Litsa replied sitting down on a large rock. Her legs were weak and she felt as though she needed to be seated for all Jeff…or Madia…was telling her.

"The secret he told you was that you would take this trip and what you had to do," Jeff told her with a gentle smile.

Litsa's eyes were tearing up. "I'll do whatever you want me to, all you have to do is tell me."

"Come now, I want to show you the entrance to our city," he smiled as he took her hand. They walked to the cliff wall across the canyon from where she had been sitting. Behind a large rock was a well concealed opening that led into the cliff. It was a small entrance and Litsa had to bend down to enter.

Once inside, she couldn't believe her eyes. Several torches were lit showing a huge room where petroglyphs and large drawings were on every wall. She felt like she was in a dream world. The drawings and petroglyphs told the story of the life and heartaches those poor souls had endured during all their years in the canyons. Litsa walked slowly so she could look at them closely. They were so full of character.

At the far end of the room there was, what appeared to be, an altar. As Madia took her by the hand again Litsa felt the same strange excitement she had felt when they were on the trail, when he held her close to him. As they drew closer to the altar Litsa could see a strangely shaped rock in the middle of it.

"This rock is the center of our universe," Madia told her. "The gold nugget you have is the key that will free our spirits."

"But why me?" Litsa said pulling the nugget out of her pocket.

"The time is ending for us here in this canyon and soon all the spirits may be bound to the underworld and not be free to go toward the stars and beyond the universe. The gold piece that you have there is the key that will set us free, but until the key is replaced we are destined to the underworld. The ancestors many years ago had told us about you, and that you were the one special mortal that could set us free."

"But you are free, you came and got me in human form," Litsa told him, her eyes full of question.

"I was made Shaman many years ago. I am the keeper of the spirits and have been free to travel and take on the human form. I traveled all over this place you call earth, from Siberia to Africa, learning the ways of all shamans, their healing and medical techniques. I learned there are many things that can help in today's world. New diseases are discovered every day like AIDS, cancers, damaged hearts, tumors. I could go on forever. Most of the cures come from right here on earth, from plants, herbs, insects. You, being a nurse, know how disturbed today's medical doctors are when they can't help a child who is suffering from a deadly disease. They want to save the child's life. And elderly people, preventing them from having pains so severe they can't move."

Litsa watched him as he spoke and thought to herself what a gentle soul he was. "I will do any thing to help you, just tell me what to do," she replied.

"First, come, I want to show you the city," he told her. "That's what you came to see. Come with me." On the far side of the altar was another small opening. As they went through it they came into another room where a small stream ran quietly along their path. "Go ahead, take a drink. You will find it's the purest water anywhere in this world."

Litsa cupped her hands and took a drink. It tasted like what spring was, new flowers, new life. She had never tasted anything like it before. It was delicious.

"Come now and I will show you more," he smiled. As they went into another room there was steam coming from small holes in the floor. Litsa could hear the sound of a waterfall.

"Put your hand into the water," Madia told her. Litsa held out her hand, putting it into the water that was coming out of the wall. It was as warm as bath water, pure and clean as could be. The room felt like an exquisite steam bath.

"This is amazing," she said laughing.

"Later this evening you may come back here and take a bath if you'd like," he told her smiling.

"I would love that," Litsa said returning the smile.

"Come now, I think the food is ready. I'm sure you are hungry," Madia said as they walked through another low opening. They went still further into the cliff city and entered a large room with woven rugs, pillows on the floor, and small tables in front of the pillows. The food was already on the tables and Litsa was overwhelmed at the spread. There was corn, beans, turkey, venison, Indian bread, honey, and it all smelled wonderful.

"One thing I need to ask," Litsa said looking around the room. "Where are the rest of the people? Will they be joining us for this incredible meal?"

Madia smiled at her. "They have been around you the whole time you've been here. They have been waiting for you for a very long time."

"I can't see them," Litsa said still searching the room.

"That's because you are mortal and they are in the spirit world. Please come sit down," Madia said patting the pillow next to him. Litsa didn't realize she was so hungry. She thought back to when Jeff first came to her door, and how he had eaten. Now she was his guest in an ancient city.

When they had finished, they sat and listened to the sound of ancient music. Madia explained that it was the music of healing that his people played in gratitude for her arrival and dedication to freeing them. After a while, he told her that her bath was ready. They returned to the room of steam and the waterfall. "There is a robe for you by the water. I'll see you when you are finished."

On a small table there was a towel, and soap she guessed was made from the yucca cactus. A large tub-like pool was in the corner looking ever so inviting and there on a rock was a beautiful soft, white robe. As she slid into the water she felt a peace she had never felt before. It was like being held in your mother's arms when you were a baby. Never had she felt so secure and content. This place was like paradise, and she hoped if this was a dream she would never wake up.

Chapter 8

As she bathed in utter relaxation her thoughts turned to what she had learned and seen at Delphi, in Greece, and she recalled the woman called Pythia. Dating back to 1400 BC, rulers of state and individuals in all parts of the world a thousand years ago approached Pythia, the Oracle of Delphi, for advice. It was called the seat of Manto, a sacred tripod where Pythia would sit while prophetic vapors emanated from deep within the ground. She would fall into a trance and become possessed by prophetic delirium, after which she would begin to pour forth prophecies. Delphi was believed to be the center of Apollo's universe. It was a fantastic place with innumerable art treasures. The Greeks would send extravagant gifts in an effort to keep the Oracle on their side. It all ended in the fourth century AD, when a new Christian Rome proscribed the Oracle's prophesying as false and misleading.

Later it was learned that the vapors from secret faults were found to have been inspired by natural gas emitted from deep within the earth's crust. The Greeks and Romans took their prophesies from a woman who was high on fumes of natural gas! These trances occasionally deepened into delirium or even death for some people. It was described as a sweet fragrance, like perfume. The speculation was that the gases came from rocks below and were affected by earthquakes, like the one in 373 BC that destroyed the cities on the Gulf of Corinth. The fumes were believed to be ethylene, a sweet smelling gas that would affect the nervous system. It was used as an anesthetic and in small doses it would produce a floating sensation and euphoria. This is just what the Oracle needed to start the visions. Litsa smiled to herself, imagining she was the Oracle.

She had just gotten out of the water and put the robe on when Madia asked to come into the room. "That was the most divine bath I have ever had!" she told him gratefully.

"I knew you would enjoy it and that it would relax you for the night. Come now, I will show you where you will sleep," Madia told her. They crossed the room and went into another, smaller room. There was a large bed on the floor with a beautifully woven cover and large pillows. Litsa was so tired she could hardly hold her eyes open. "Sleep well. I will see you in the morning," then he kissed her on the forehead and left."

The sun's rays woke Litsa in the morning as they shined through tiny holes in the cliff wall. They made the whole room light up. She sat up, and to her surprise, saw the most beautiful white squaw dress lying next to her. It had a beaded headband with silver and gold, a matching belt, and white moccasins with the same design on them. The dress was of what appeared to be deer hide, exceptionally soft and velvety. She shook her head in amazement.

In the corner was a small bathroom and on a table with a stone bowl of water for washing up was a small rectangular piece of shiny silver for a mirror. A comb, like she had never seen before, made of animal bone was next to it. On a tray near the clothes were a piece of Indian bread and some hot tea. She didn't know who had left it but she was more than grateful.

Slipping the dress and moccasins on, it seemed as if they had been made just for her. She felt like an Indian princess, but why her? She was Greek. How did she fit into this whole scheme of things, she wondered. Just then she heard Madia calling her name and she walked out into the next room to find him standing there, looking more handsome than any man she had ever seen.

"You look beautiful," Madia said. "I trust you had a good night's rest."

"Better than any I can ever remember," Litsa told him smiling.

"I want to show you something," he told her. "Come with me."

As she followed him, going to the far corner of the room, she saw a tiny entrance, which led into a most beautiful garden. It wasn't large but beautifully landscaped with a small brook running through it. There were flowers of every color and a path that went all the way around it. Madia took Litsa's hand as they walked along the path. He told her the time was drawing near, and how much he wanted to thank her for her help.

"May I ask a question?" Litsa said. "I really don't understand all of this. I'm Greek. Why on earth did you, or your people, choose me?"

"It doesn't matter what background you came from, it's where your heart is that matters," Madia told her. "You were chosen when you were born, the one the elders said would be the mortal who would release our spirits."

Litsa felt a tear running down her cheek. Madia turned to face her, and gently wiped the tear away. "Will I ever see you again?" Litsa asked him. He put his hand under her ear, running his fingers through her hair, then to the back of her head, pulling her close to him. The excitement she felt as he pressed his lips to hers was beyond description. In that moment their souls were united as one. It felt like their spirits had joined together, flying higher and higher into the sky above, racing toward the stars. Then they felt as if they were flying faster and faster and a sense of ecstasy beyond words encompassed them. Then slowly, they were coming back down, returning to earth. Litsa never wanted the feeling to end. This time he didn't push her away, but held her tightly. They stood there holding each other, not wanting to ever let go.

Finally, Madia told Litsa, "I must explain to you the reason you are here." Taking her by the hand they walked over to a bench made of stone in the garden. "Please sit," Madia said. "You see, you were the chosen one partly because of your heritage. The Greeks had endured many hardships for thousands of years, through many wars, and still they never gave up. They were a very brilliant culture and gave the world great bounty in literature and art. Greeks also gave birth to the Olympics, which to this day are still held for the whole world to enjoy. These are just some of the aspects of who you are, being Greek, that signify why you were chosen."

"I have many things to teach you and only a short time in which to do it. The things I teach you and those you see will vastly help all the people in the world. In time you will be able to use the information I give you." Litsa had a puzzled look on her face, but he told her, "You will understand more as time goes on. For now, just trust me and learn as I teach."

Madia went on to tell her about the legend of an evil force at work in the world. "He is known as 'Jalousie', the word for jealous, and he wanted control over the entire universe." He explained to her that many thousands of years ago Jalousie was a great warrior in a beautiful country that is now part of South America. He lost a battle for a beautiful lady and the right to rule the world, thus he was put to shame and cast out. Ever since then he has made trouble with numerous countries and civilizations causing many to cease in existence. It was his desire to destroy all traces of the human population in his anger."

"Jalousie was the cause for the disappearance of the ancient Mayans, who vanished around 600 BC, and left only ruins. The Incan people, who had built a large civilization in Peru, disappeared leaving minimal traces of their existence. The ancient Civilization of Tiahuanaco, also known as Tiwanaku in Bolivian Andes also mysteriously disappeared around 1200 A.D., and the people of Easter Island vanished leaving only stone ruins. Then there were the Nazca Indians, the ones who left the giant drawings of creatures and trapezoids over a large area on the pampas of Peru. Jalousie caused the collapse of the Roman Empire, and obliterated Atlantis, which disappeared without a trace, plus many more instances of destruction and annihilation. He is an evil force that wants to destroy the whole world.

"As he moved about the universe he tried to destroy the Anasazi people. He caused hardships and death to my people driving us underground. He tried to destroy us by putting a curse on us that if we didn't find someone to release our spirits in a thousand years that our souls would forever be bound to the underground world. But there is also a good force and Jalousie feared someday he would be defeated and our curse would be lifted."

"There were documents made long ago that were found in the ruins of Kalasasaya temple in Tiahuanaco which tell of the ways to find everlasting love and inner-peace and how an evil force could be destroyed. Jalousie knew that if these were ever discovered his powers could be destroyed and he would be banished from this earth forever. The gold key your grandfather gave you came from a Celestine temple in Peru with instructions for banishing the curse on my people."

Madia stood and turned to Litsa saying, "This is the reason you are here. You are the one that was chosen many years ago according to the documents to release our spirits and to destroy Jalouise's curse forever. There is a legend conspicuous in the Hopi Indians, about the Finnish Kalevala epic that came from the Mayan and Aztec calendars, predicts that all civilizations will be destroyed by "Nahuati Olin" (earthquakes). That is to be Jalouise's last reign of terror here on earth. When the documents were found in Peru it told how to destroy Jalouise and his powers, and to free our spirits that were bound here on earth".

Chapter 9

Slowly they walked back into the city. "I want to show you the rest of the city," Madia said going to the far side of the main room. Near the altar he pushed a small stone and the wall began to move. Litsa's eyes grew wide with surprise as they entered the expansive caverns of the city. They went from one large area to the next. Some were surrounded with clay rooms built around the edges. Madia explained that they were the living quarters of the people. There was a grand ceremonial area with circular pits called kivas where sacred rites had been performed by the holy men of the tribe. Many petroglyphs and extensive artwork covered the walls. All of the places he showed her were still in excellent condition, even though it had been many centuries since the people had lived there.

"This is virtually all that is left of my people to show that we were ever on this earth. Only a small number survived the calamities and merged with other tribes such as the Hopi and Zuni."

"I was chosen as Shaman many years ago to protect the lost city and the spirits that are here. Now their time is running out, the thousand years will end in a few days and there is still much to teach you. I want to share with you our knowledge of nature and healing medicines, and many other things about the past and things that are yet to come."

Madia talked for hours with Litsa listening to every word he said. He told her about remedies that would cure many afflictions including the cold, pneumonia, flu virus, and those that would help the new strains of virus that would plague the world. He also advised her regarding medicines for leukemia and cancers, especially focusing on those for children.

Madia had shared with Litsa many aspects of the world his people had known, and secrets of how he worked with animals and made them do as he commanded. He told her about the stars and the ways his people had used them to map out roads and know when the seasons would start and end.

After the fifth day Litsa had begun to notice a change was taking place in Madia. He seemed to be aging rapidly and his hair was beginning to turn white as his body grew older by the hour. It had been nearly a week since they entered the city and she had been a good student absorbing everything Madia had told her. He was easy to listen to and he conveyed a bounty of pertinent information that answered her many questions about his people.

"I need to tell you one more thing to be cautious about," he told her.

"What is that?" Litsa asked.

"Remember, I told you about Jalousie, that he will try and destroy you too, because by you releasing our spirits that will also banish the curse and end his terror here on earth. He will try and stop you, but once you make it out of the canyon he can't harm you or my people ever again. I will not be there to protect you. You must make the trip back alone. Be wise and alert, but know he is limited in his power over you. Most of his powers will be gone after you free my people, but you must be cautious as you depart this canyon. He will surely have one last effort in his anger."

Litsa realized she had a huge responsibility to the Anasazi people, but she also knew without a doubt she could do it, or she would die trying. The following day, as they walked around the garden Madia told her the secrets of his past and of things that were yet to take place. By this time he appeared to have aged extremely. His hair had turned completely white, and his body was that of a very old man. Litsa had to hold his arm to help him walk.

It was almost noon and Madia and Litsa had been in the garden all morning when, in the distance, Litsa heard the faint beating of drums. Madia said, "The time has come, the ceremony has begun." They walked back through the cavern and into the main room toward the altar.

Madia now was in old age and needed Litsa to help him up onto the large stone. It made him look like a statue. "Now is the time, Litsa," he said in a strange, lilting voice.

She stood there watching him filled with a myriad of emotions. She knew what she had to do, and it was breaking her heart to have to let him go. He was starting to fade away like he had done when they first arrived. Suddenly there was a flash of lightning that struck the cavern and jolted them severely.

"Quickly, Litsa!" she heard Madia saying as he was fading into space. She urgently ran to put the golden key in its place on the rock altar. The moment it was in place, she looked up and saw spirits going through the cavern ceiling, hundreds of them. Then she turned and saw that Madia was gone. In what seemed like only a few moments they had all disappeared and she was totally alone. Litsa couldn't hold the tears back and she dropped down on her knees and wept. The sense of losing the gentlest man she had ever known tore at her heart, but she knew she had done the right thing for him and all his people.

The ground began to shake and, in a panic, Litsa rose and sprinted to the main entrance of the cave and out into the sun. Immediately she saw Benny waiting for her. He had his packs on with all her belongings, so she quickly changed her clothes and carefully packed the dress and moccasins away. As she took Benny's lead rope she knew it was going to be a long, dangerous trip back, and this time she would be going alone without any help.

As she hurried along down the trail her mind went over everything she had been through the past few weeks. She was sad, yet felt joy at the same time, knowing that she had done what she was meant to do. Now she knew she had to get home. The thought of telling Gus the story of all she had seen and done made her smile, but would he believe her? It would sound extremely strange, she had no doubt, but thinking what Madia had told her about Jalousie made chills run through her veins, and the end of the canyon was a long ways out. And Madia…she knew she would never be the same again having been with him and knowing what a wonderful man he was.

She said a prayer to her God, and kissing the cross she wore around her neck asked for his help and protection. With Benny in tow she swiftly headed toward the mouth of the Dark Canyon intent on escaping as quickly and safely as possible.

Behind her she heard the frightening sound of a huge blast. The ground trembled and suddenly rocks started falling from the cliff where she had entered the city. She began to run pulling Benny behind her. Rocks were falling everywhere around her and closing the path behind her. She was yelling at Benny to hurry as she dodged one rock after another, then a large rock came crashing down and hit Litsa from the side, knocking her down. She fell to the side of the trail as more rocks rolled on by her. Then as quickly as it had begun, it ended, and an eerie silence surrounded her. She still had

Benny's lead rope locked in her grip and he was moving around nervously waiting for her to get up, but she was in shock and awe from the landslide and couldn't move.

After a few moments she felt excruciating pain and was afraid she was going to pass out. As she waited for her head to clear, she checked to find out how badly she had been injured. She had some scrapes on her arms and knew her hip was going to be bruised, but then she felt immense pain in her ankle. She eased out of her boot and saw it was bleeding. It definitely did not look good. She knew she had to get up and keep going and get out of the canyon before anything else happened. Pulling herself up by holding onto Benny, she became certain that her ankle was broken. It wouldn't hold her weight and was turned in an awkward position. She opened the pack and grabbed a shirt that she could use, tore it, and wrapped her ankle until she could stop and tend to it better.

Benny was extremely nervous and kept pulling at his rope. Litsa held on for dear life knowing that she was in great danger as the ground trembled again. She hung on tightly to Benny and let him help her as determination overcame pain. She was resolved in not letting Jalousie destroy her.

Fifty feet down the trail, Litsa could no longer hold on. Letting go, she tumbled down a little hill knocking herself unconscious. Benny stood over her to protect her. When she started to come around, Benny nuzzled her gently with his nose while she lay there waiting for her head to clear. She no longer could hear falling rocks, but when she started to move the pain from her ankle made her cry out. She knew she had to get help, but from where? No one knew where she was. Her mother knew she had gone to Dark Canyon, but that was very little considering how large an area it was and how long it had taken them to get there. Only her grandfather knew and he couldn't help. She knew her life hung in the balance with only Benny there to help.

Litsa remembered Madia saying something about an outpost being ten miles from the canyon. She knew she had to make it there to get help, but how? She couldn't walk and Benny was a pack mule. Would he let her ride? Pulling herself up by hanging onto Benny for all she was worth, she remembered there was pain medicine in the packs. Digging through for the first aid kit, she found the old map. She was grateful for that because there were all kinds of different little canyons that went nowhere and, if she got into one of them, it could take days for her to escape the area. The map would help her find the right one to get her out of Dark Canyon.

Finding the pain pills, she took two and a drink from the canteen. Someone had filled it with water from the city. She remembered the delicious taste. Thinking back, she wondered how she could have been so happy in the city, and here in such pain. And now she was totally alone, except for Benny. The range of emotions was more than she could handle and she began to cry.

"No, Litsa!" she said to herself. "Cowgirl up! You have to get yourself together and get out of here." She sat for a few minutes to let the pain pills begin to work, then leading Benny over to a small hill she got on the high side and slid over on Benny's back talking softly to him to encourage his patience. Benny laid his ears back and Litsa held her breath, wondering if he would cooperate or dump her off. With only a lead rope she would not have much control over where he went. She clicked at him and he started on down the trail acting as if this was not a major event. If he had never carried a human before it was his secret. For some reason though, it was as if he understood his mission and was content to carry on.

After a short time Litsa could feel the pain pills taking affect. Her head was feeling better but the ankle was throbbing from hanging down so she tried putting it up over the pack and that helped some. An hour had gone by and Litsa started to wonder if they were following the right trail. By that time the afternoon sun was shining brightly into the canyon making it so hot she could hardly breathe.

Benny, up to this point, had done very well. Litsa thought that by talking to him, perhaps it would put him more at ease, and she would be able to get her mind off her pain. After what seemed like hours, she had told Benny everything that had happened to her. As she patted him on the neck, his long ears would move to every word she said as if he understood, and he was taking each step with care. It was as if he knew he had an important mission and was trying his best not to slip and make Litsa fall again. Maybe some of what Madia had told Litsa about animals was working on Benny.

After about three hours Litsa saw a big curve ahead in the canyon. She was hoping that around that curve was where they had left Starlight and Favorito, and that they would still be there. Sure enough, following the curve and down a small hill she heard one of the horses whinny. She let out a big sigh knowing they were still there. As they came around to where Litsa could see both the horses staring up the trail at them she said, "I knew I could count on you two!"

The afternoon was turning into long shadows and she knew she was going to have to make camp soon. She steered Benny over to a small hill and slid off him trying to keep her balance, but was on loose rock and began slipping until she tumbled right under Benny again. He stood there while she got back up holding on to him. "Benny, that's another bucket of grain for you," Litsa said, rubbing his neck.

Seeing a branch of cottonwood about twenty feet away, it looked like something Litsa could use as a crutch. Crawling on her hands and one good foot she managed to get to it. Lifting herself up and holding on to the branch she heard a crack, then it broke making her fall again. She sat on the ground angry with herself for getting into this situation. She was only a few yards from the small spring so carefully she crawled over to the water. Taking the rag off her ankle she put her foot into the cool water. For a moment it took her breath away, then it started to feel better.

Looking around she saw another branch on the other side of the spring. This time she hoped it would be stronger and not break under her weight, but for the moment the cool water felt too good to leave.

After soaking her foot for about twenty minutes she thought she had better get a fire started. Looking around she saw that Benny was grazing about fifty feet away. In the packs Benny was carrying were the matches. Taking her foot out of the water, she dried it and wrapped it again in the shirt she'd had on it. The ankle had swollen and was painful and there was no way she could get her boot on it. She would have to continue with only the shirt wrapped around it. If she could get to the branch, she thought, she could at least get to Benny. The only problem was the branch was on the other side of the little spring. This time, on her hands and one good foot, she tried to jump the spring like an animal, landing on the far side in the mud. Her hands slid out from under her making her land face down in the mud.

Coughing and spitting mud out of her mouth she thought to herself, well at least you made it, but you sure wouldn't make a good animal. That at least brought a grin to her face. She saw the branch was about ten feet away, so she crawled over to it hoping this one might do the job for her. She pulled herself up again slowly, waiting to see if this one would break. It didn't and she sighed in relief. She returned to the spring to wash off the mud and the cool water felt refreshing.

Looking around now for Benny, she discovered he had moved to the little hill on the other side of the spring. As mules will do, he was grazing on a hill so he wouldn't have to reach so far for his food. How was she going to get to him? She'd had enough problems just getting to the branch. The pain pills were starting to wear off and her ankle was beginning to throb again. She knew she had to get to Benny to get the first aid kit. The cuts and bruises she had from the rock hitting her, plus those from her falls since then, were getting sore and needed attention. She really needed that first aid kit to treat everything.

She noticed Favorito had been standing and watching her closely since she had found him and Starlight. Holding out her hand to Favorito and calling to him brought him right up to her. Thank goodness she had left his halter on.

"Good boy! I knew I could count on you," she told him with a smile. He nuzzled her face and searched her for a treat. "Careful Favorito, you'll knock me down again," she said wearily.

Chapter 10

The sun was nearly down now and shadows consumed the canyon she was in. Taking her belt off, Litsa put it though Favorito's halter, then hopped over to a rock she could crawl up on, pulling the horse alongside. She slid onto his back and turned him toward the spring, crossing it and moving over to where Benny was eating. She reached into the pack and found the first aid kit with the pain pills, matches, and some dried beef her mother insisted she bring along.

Thinking back she remembered Jeff had left the saddles on the far side of the little meadow in a cave. "I could sure use the warmth of one of those saddle blankets for the night," she said to Favorito. Making their way back across the spring to where the saddles were, she slid off the horse holding onto the belt. Reaching for one of the lead ropes, she hooked it to Favorito's halter and let it drop. She could at least count on him to stay there, as he had been trained to stay in one place with his reins dropped on the ground.

Crawling into the little cave, she took the pain pills and ate some dried beef. Wrapping the blanket around her, she leaned against the rock wall and soon drifted off to sleep, too tired to even start a fire. During the night she was awakened a couple of times feeling like something was watching her. Favorito seems to be a bit nervous too, she thought, but exhaustion was greater than her fear and she swiftly went back to sleep.

Litsa was glad to see the sun's early morning rays drift into the canyon. Crawling out of the cave she felt the warmth of the sun. Never had it felt so good. Her ankle was now in a lot of pain though, so she looked around and spotted a small stick she could break and use as splints. She put one on either side of her ankle then tied Starlight's lead rope around it to make the ankle more stable. As swollen and painful as it was, she was amazed at how well she was enduring the misery.

Eating the rest of the dried beef and taking a couple more pain pills, she crawled over to Favorito, then stood and led him over to the saddles hopping on her good foot. She threw the saddle blanket on him, then struggling and hopping, finally got him saddled. She left Starlight's saddle in the cave hoping she would get back for it in a week or so. She wanted to make it to the outpost sometime that day if at all possible. Already her efforts were wearing on her.

Crossing the spring and moving onto the trail, she started out of the canyon with Starlight and Benny randomly following behind her. Moving toward the opening of the canyon, she saw the sides were not as steep and the area around her was more of rolling hills with juniper and pinion trees and low hanging cliffs. She hoped she would be safe from the Jalousie curse, but she was not out of the canyon yet.

With Benny behind her and Starlight bringing up the rear she traveled slowly, but was grateful that she had the horses and everything together again. Suddenly she heard Starlight let out the most terrorizing sound she had ever heard. When she turned she saw a cougar had landed right on his back from the low hanging cliff she had just passed under.

Starlight was screaming and trying to buck him off. Benny went running past her almost causing Favorito to lose his footing. Litsa was reaching in her saddlebags hunting for the .38 pistol she had there. Turning, she fired one shot missing the cougar, but with second and third shots she knew she had hit the cat. Starlight was rearing and bucking harder to get the cougar off him, and finally the cougar lost his death grip and fell.

Just at that moment she saw a huge blast of light like a fireball and a horrifying scream coming from deep inside the canyon. The sound made echoes that bounced off the canyon walls for several moments. Favorito spun around in terror and she held on for dear life. Benny was nowhere in sight and Starlight was running straight toward them with eyes showing tremendous fear. She realized in a heartbeat that Jalousie was defeated, but didn't know how she would survive the terror he had just subjected them to. She jerked Favorito's reins and went after Starlight, yelling for Benny at the same time. She was in such panic that her ankle was the least of her worries.

Litsa's heart was pounding as she urged Favorito closer to Starlight. He was bleeding from a deep gash on his shoulder the cat had made. She spoke to him the way Madia had taught her and soon Starlight slowed to a walk. She pulled Favorito up next to him taking the lead rope off her ankle, hooked it to his halter, then led him back to some trees near the dead cougar. Starlight was prancing around in a nervous fit and she spoke to him to calm him down. She tied him to a branch, then went back to examine the cat. She could see blood coming from a wound on the cougar's head where one bullet had hit him between his ear and eye killing him instantly.

Favorito was snorting and acting very nervous, so she turned him back toward where Starlight was tied, but trying to pull loose in panic. Well, she thought to herself, if the cat was part of the Jalousie curse that won't happen again! She untied Starlight, looking to see where Benny was, but knowing he may still be running. While she tried to get Starlight to settle down she realized she had to get help, but how far was the outpost, she wondered. It looked like Starlight was losing a lot of blood where the cougar had made the gash with his claw.

Litsa leaned over and spoke to him softly telling him everything would be okay now, and looking closer at the gash on his shoulder. It was not as deep as she thought. He was lucky, as it was just under the skin but not into any muscle area. Litsa was grateful for that. Looking around she noticed she was only a few yards from the opening of the canyon where Jeff and she had entered.

Coming out of the canyon and into flat land, Litsa saw Benny grazing about fifty feet from the trail. When he saw them approaching he started to bray loudly. Moving alongside him she reached for his lead rope. She pulled Starlight up beside Benny and tied the rope to Benny's packsaddle. She took Benny's rope and finally felt she had things under control.

Looking around she saw that she was finally out of the canyon and the trail was climbing toward the south. At last she knew for certain she was no longer in danger from Jalousie. Now Madia and the rest of the world would never have to fear his curse again, she had done her job and done it with a brave heart.

Litsa's eyes filled with tears of joy, but of sadness too, knowing that Madia was gone. He was a man she could have fallen in love with and been happy for the rest of her life. Memories of him filled her mind as her heart ached from losing him. But she also had a sense of knowing that she had done what she was born to do.

By that time, her ankle was starting to ache violently and she felt weak and feverish. Benny, when he took off running, had somehow knocked the canteen off his pack so there was no water to drink or pour onto Starlight's shoulder. All she could hope for now was that she was close to the outpost.

After what seemed like a couple of hours, they finally came upon a trail that looked as though it had been used as an ATV road a few times. In Litsa's foggy head she knew that would be a trail to follow. This trail might lead to a better road, she thought. They followed the trail for about a mile where it turned into a dirt road, one that might have been a Forest Service road. It was about five o'clock in the afternoon when Litsa and the horses came up and out onto a ridge.

Looking off into the distance she saw what she thought looked like some kind of building. She now had a burning fever and the ankle was throbbing in terrific pain. Making her way down the hill onto the flat land, she could feel herself starting to black out. Starlight was pulling back and she knew he was also in pain, but they had to keep moving.

Dropping Benny's lead rope and trying to just hang on, Litsa was slipping into unconsciousness. She was trying hard to keep going and all she could do now was let Favorito have his head and hope he would lead her to help.

Chapter 11

At the Needles Outpost, Tracey and Gary were cleaning up after a busy day. People were coming to spend the night at the campgrounds and buying a few groceries, things they'd forgotten to pack. Kids were climbing the rocks in back of the outpost while a few small planes flew in and out from the dirt runway nearby. Everything seemed like it was normal when someone came running in the door yelling, "There's a lady and horses coming in and it looks like they need help."

Tracey went running and saw Litsa slumped over the saddle with the mule and horse behind her. One horse had blood all over his shoulder and running down his front leg.

"Get Gary", Tracey hollered. "Tell him to call for help at the Sheriff's office in Monticello! Tell him to hurry!"

When Favorito was almost to the porch of the office, Gary and a tourist were there to get Litsa down. "Looks like her ankle is broken, it's badly swollen. Careful with her, lets take her inside," Gary instructed as they carried her into the store to the back room where they had a cot. "Go get some water, ice and a towel. It looks like this lady has really gotten herself into trouble," Gary said.

Litsa started to come around just long enough to know she had made it to the outpost. Then she went unconscious again. "She is burning up with fever," Tracey said. " I wonder what happened?"

Leaving Litsa in Tracey's care, Gary went back out to see what he could do for the horses. He took the packs off Benny and the saddle off Favorito then looked at the gash on Starlight's front shoulder.

"Whoa, big guy! I just need to take a look," he said as he approached Starlight and led him to the drinking trough. "It's not too bad. A little bit of water to clean this off and we'll get you fixed right up. Your mistress doesn't look so good though. You guys have had a run in with something bad," he said thoughtfully.

It was about a half hour before Sheriff Johnson got to the outpost. "Did you get her name?" the Sheriff asked when he saw Litsa lying on the cot.

"She came to for just a few moments and said her name was Litsa," Tracey told him. "That's all we know."

The Sheriff went into the other room to make a phone call. Tracey had been tending to Litsa, trying to bring her fever down and clean her up a bit. Just then, Gary came in from tending the horses and Benny.

"That black horse has some wounds. Looks like he might have encountered a mountain lion. We've got him in the corral and the vet is on his way over. Doesn't look too bad, though. Wonder where the heck this gal has been?" he said to Tracey.

After a few minutes the Sheriff returned to where Gary and Tracey were talking. "A bulletin came out this morning from the Sheriff's office in Grand Junction, Colorado. Her mother, Sophia, who lives in Grand Junction, was worried about her daughter, Litsa. She's been gone for nearly three weeks and the mother had not heard a thing from her. I guess her plans were that she was only going to be camping in the Dark Canyon area for about a week or so," the Sheriff told them.

"I'll get in touch with the hospital in Grand Junction and have them fly their helicopter over here and pick her up. Also, I'll have the Sheriff's office put in a call to her mother. Gary, did you check the injuries to that horse?" the Sheriff asked looking out the window toward the corral.

"Yes, the vet will be up in an hour or so," Gary replied.

"From that gash on his shoulder it looks like maybe a cougar attacked him," the Sheriff said nodding toward the horses.

The helicopter from Grand Junction landed at the Needles Outpost about two hours after the Sheriff had called. While Tracey was tending Litsa keeping a cool washcloth on her head, she would briefly open her eyes and try to speak, but few words were coming out. Tracey just put her finger to her lips and made a shhhh sound, then Litsa drifted off again.

The medical team from the helicopter had Litsa prepared and on board quickly, and told Tracey it would take about thirty minutes to fly her to Grand Junction. By this time a crowd of people had gathered around the Outpost office wondering what all the excitement was about. Gary stepped outside and told them just a little about Litsa coming there and that everything was under control.

"The lady will be fine. They're taking her up to Grand Junction now," he informed them.

Gary and Tracey went back inside the small store after the helicopter was gone. "I wonder if she was involved with that noise we heard yesterday. Might have been a rock slide or somebody blasting back in those canyons," Gary said.

About that time Dr. Bell pulled up at the store. "I hear you had a little trouble here," he said to Gary.

"Yep, the horse is in the back," Gary told him. "He has a mean-looking gash on his shoulder."

Dr. Bell looked Starlight over. "Looks like a cougar attacked him," he said after a few minutes. "The cut doesn't look too bad. I'll clean it up and put a few stitches in there and he'll be fine in a day or two. Who does he belong to?"

"A lady came in riding that horse over there," Gary told him pointing to Favorito. "She was in pretty bad shape with a broken ankle and cuts and bruises all over her body. A medical helicopter from Grand Junction picked her up a little while ago.

"Was she able to tell you what had happened"? Dr. Bell asked.

"Not much. She said something about a rockslide, and having to get out of the canyon and away from an evil force. It could've been the fever playing tricks on her mind," Gary told him as they walked back toward the office.

I'll come back up in a few days and check on the horse. He's a good looking animal. I don't think that gash will leave much of a scar on his shoulder."

Two days later, when Dr. Bell came back to the Outpost to check on Starlight, Tracey was had just come from the corral. "How is he doing today?" Dr. Bell asked.

"Much better," Tracey told him. "The owners called yesterday and said they'll be here this afternoon to pick them all up. I guess they belong to a sheep rancher in Grand Junction."

Chapter 12

"I think she's starting to wake up," the nurse said to Litsa's mother. Sophia had been sitting by her daughter's hospital bed since the helicopter brought her in the day before. "We finally got her fever down and the infection seems to be clearing up. She's a very lucky lady. She will have to have surgery on that ankle when she feels better, but for right now she just needs to rest.

"Where am I?" Litsa asked as she awoke. Turning her head she saw her mother sitting beside her. "Oh mother! I'm so glad to see you!"

Sophia's hand gripped Litsa's as she asked, "What happened out there?"

"I'll tell you later," Litsa said. "First tell me how I got here, and how is Grandfather doing? I must talk to him. Where are the horses? How is Starlight?"

"Hold on, not so fast young lady!" Sophia told her gently. "You apparently had quite a traumatic experience out there in the canyons."

"I need to know how Grandfather is," Litsa said almost crying.

"He's doing much better now, but he doesn't know about you being in the hospital," Sophia told her. "I didn't want to upset him any more than he already was. He called me every day you were gone to see if I had heard any word from you. He said some strange things about a guy you were to meet at Newspaper Rock in Utah. He said he knew the guy and that you would be safe with him and I shouldn't worry. Well, when you didn't come back after more than a week I started to really get worried, so I notified the Sheriff's office."

"Mother, how long was I gone?" Litsa asked.

"A little over two weeks ," Sophia told her.

"I guess I lost all track of time," Litsa said shaking her head. The nurse had given her an injection to help her remain calm and as it began to take affect, Litsa started to drift off to sleep again.

"The doctor will be in to check on her in a few minutes. She's a very brave lady, and very lucky," the nurse told Sophia . "Whatever happened to her must have been quite frightening. She talked a lot about someone named Madia, rambling on about how she was going to miss him. She would almost scream out saying, 'No, don't go!' What do you think that was all about?" the nurse said to Sophia.

"I'm sure we will get to the bottom of this when she feels better," Sophia said. She sat quietly by Litsa's side and then looked up to see a doctor come into the room. She hadn't seen him before but his presence commanded respect. Sophia just stared up at him thinking what a handsome man he was.

"I would like to check your daughter if you could step outside for a few minutes," he told her with a gentle smile.

"Of course," Sophia said. Seeing the nurse, Sophia asked her about the doctor that was checking Litsa.

"He's a new doctor here. He started about a week ago and has a long line of degrees that make him very qualified to be here," she responded smiling. "We are quite proud that he chose our hospital to come to."

The next morning Litsa was getting prepped for surgery on her ankle. "Mother, will you be here when I get back?" she asked Sophia.

"Of course, darling," Sophia said. "I also want to see that doctor again."

"What doctor?" Litsa asked.

"Why, your doctor," Sophia said with a strange look on her face. "Haven't you met him yet?"

"I guess not," Litsa said curiously. "You can tell me about him after the surgery."

About that time the nurses aides came in the door with a gurney. "Are you ready, Litsa?"

"Yes I am!" she said firmly. "I want to get this ankle fixed so I can get on my feet again."

As they entered the operating room, Litsa was overcome with a strange feeling. The nurse leaned over and said, "This is your doctor."

Litsa was slowly drifting away when she caught sight of the doctor with his mask on. Those eyes, she thought. Where have I seen them? With that the anesthetic overpowered her and she drifted into a peaceful sleep.

Two hours later they wheeled Litsa into the recovery room. "She will be fine now," the doctor said. "I'll go talk to her mother."

He found Sophia waiting in the lobby and told her, "Your daughter is going to be fine. We had to put a pin into the bone, but with some therapy she should be up and walking very soon. She is a strong, lovely young lady. Did she tell you how this happened?"

"I don't have the full story yet," Sophia replied. "It has to do with coming out of Dark Canyon and a rock that came crashing down hitting her on the ankle. Then a cougar attacked one of her horses. Thank goodness she knew how to handle a gun. The folks at the Needles Outpost said she shot the cougar in the head and killed him, probably saving her grandfather's horse.

It sounds like an interesting story," he said nodding. "I will see her later," he smiled and left the room.

Thirty minutes later they brought Litsa back to her room. She was still a bit groggy but happy to have the surgery done. "Mother, did the doctor come and talk to you?" Litsa asked when her head had cleared.

"He said he would be in to talk to you later," Sophia told her.

"Mother, I think you can go home now, and please call Grandfather and tell him I will be over to see him as soon as the doctor lets me out of here. I have an incredible story to tell him."

"He knows you're here and sends his blessing," Sophia said giving her a gentle hug. "Now you get some rest."

Two days later the nurse came in and said, "Well Litsa you can go home now. Your doctor had to leave on an emergency to the hospital at Shiprock, New Mexico. He signed your papers before he left, so you could be released. Dr. Cohen will give you one last check-up before you leave."

Litsa couldn't wait to call her mother. Sophia was thrilled that Litsa and Gus were both coming home on the same day. "I'll be right over to get you," she said. When she got to the hospital Litsa was waiting at the front door in a wheelchair, ready to go.

"Mother did you say Grandfather was coming home today? I can't wait to see him," Litsa said smiling brightly. "I have a ton of things to tell him about."

Litsa was happy to be back home, and the first thing she wanted to see was if Starlight, Favorito, and Benny were all right. She had her mother drive over to the pasture and park so she could hobble to the fence with her crutches. Favorito came right up to her and she hugged him and whispered to him, "Thank you for being such a great friend." He nuzzled her with his nose then went back to grazing. She looked closely at the wound on Starlight's shoulder and saw that it had been treated well and was looking very good. She patted him on the forehead and looked for Benny. He didn't come to the fence so she waved to him and hollered, "Thanks, Benny!"

After she got into the house and got settled, she had a lunch that would be fit for royalty. Sophia knew Litsa was hungry for some good food, so she had made up a nice big lunch for her. Just as she finished eating she heard a car pull up outside. Seeing Gus in the car, she grabbed her crutches and headed for the door. "Grandfather!" she shouted as she stepped out to the front porch, and waited to give him the biggest hug ever. "I'm so glad to have you back home Grandfather. I have so much to tell you," she said struggling with her crutches.

"All in good time," Sophia said, and to Gus she said, "There's plenty of food for lunch. Come and eat." Litsa sat down at the table with him and they shared about their stays in the hospital and how Gus was doing, overall.

"Your grandfather needs to get some rest now," Sophia told Litsa. "A nap would be a good idea, I think."

Gus agreed and went to his room, telling Litsa they would talk more later. The next few days Litsa visited with him and told him all the things that had taken place from the moment she left home until she finally got to the Needles Outpost. She was baffled by the way her grandfather seemed not to recall just who Jeff was, but he was very interested in her lively story.

Two months had gone by, and it was about time to bring the sheep down from the high country and start moving them to the winter grounds in Utah. Litsa had put away her adventure in Dark Canyon, and was busy trying to get back into work at the ranch and thinking about what to do with the rest of her life. Her ankle was healing nicely and the cast was off, so she was getting around quite well.

Gus had been getting restless the past few days so at dinner one evening he told Litsa, "I'm going up to Hubbard Creek tomorrow to check on the progress of the sheep. How would you like to go riding up there? I can have Marty load Favorito for you." Marty was Gus's Spanish Basque foreman, who had been with the outfit for twelve years. He was the hardest working man in the whole outfit. "The trees are starting to turn colors and it will be a beautiful day for a ride," Gus told her with a smile.

"I would love that Grandfather, thank you." Litsa hadn't noticed she had been a bit moody lately, fussing about little things and nearly biting everyone's head off. Even Sophia agreed it would do Litsa good to get away for the day.

The ride to Paonia was quiet, neither Gus nor Litsa talked much. Turning up into Steven Gulch, Litsa could see the changing colors on the scrub oaks and as they went higher, the aspen were changing. Some were still green while others were shimmering in golden color. The sky was bright blue and it was a beautiful fall day for a ride. Litsa unloaded Favorito, then tightened the cinch and put the hackamore on and he was ready to go.

She turned him up the trail to the north side hollering to Gus that she would be back in a couple of hours. He waved, smiling, and knowing she needed to spend the time with her horse in the beauty and freedom of the mountains. As she rode along she began to think of the adventure at Dark Canyon and spoke to Favorito about it as though he understood every word. Tears finally came when she talked about Jeff and how she had felt about him.

She told Favorito what she dreamed could have been, and wondered if she would ever forget him.

Litsa pulled Favorito to a stop and dismounted letting him take a long cool drink. He wandered over to a nice green spot of grass in the small meadow and went about grazing. Litsa sat down in the tall grass and pulled a blade of grass apart to chew on. She loved the taste of the fresh grass. Laying back and looking up at the clear blue afternoon sky, she let her eyes close and soon drifted off to sleep. In a dream she saw Jeff standing in the tall grass in the middle of the meadow. She ran into his waiting arms. He looked more handsome than when she had seen him in the Dark Canyon. He held her face in his hands, looking deep into her eyes, then kissed her on the forehead. "Litsa my darling remember my love for you." Then he was gone.

Litsa awoke with a startled jolt and sat up trying to focus her eyes and clear her head. Looking around she saw Favorito still grazing in the same place, "I must have been more tired then I thought," she said to herself. "Come on big guy, we'd better get back. Grandfather will wonder where we are."

Gus and Litsa pulled into the yard late that evening. Litsa put Favorito out to pasture, then went into the house where Sophia had dinner waiting for them. "Man, am I hungry!" Litsa exclaimed.

"I trust you two had a good day?" Sophia asked as she sat down.

"Oh, Mother! The fall colors were more vibrant than I have ever seen them. We had a wonderful ride," she said as she ate heartily.

"Oh by the way, Litsa. Your doctor called today and wanted to know if it would be alright to come by tomorrow and check your ankle," Sophia told her.

"Sure, that's fine Mother," she said. Giving it no more thought, Litsa headed upstairs for a warm bath. Sleep came quickly that night, and she dreamt of Jeff and her riding in the sky among the stars.

Early the next morning, Litsa came down for a cup of coffee and toast. Sophia was in the kitchen having a cup of tea and reading the paper. "Did the doctor say what time he would be here this morning?" Litsa asked.

"No, he didn't say what time, but I hope it's the same doctor that performed your surgery."

"What did you say he looked like, again?" The tone in Litsa's voice became suddenly intense.

"Well, he had dark hair and a handsome smile, with a dimple on one side. His eyes were...well...I guess deep would describe them. He was very good looking," Sophia told her as she leafed through the paper.

A look of shock crossed Litsa's face and she bolted from the kitchen heading for the stairs. She hurried into Sophia's office and began going through the hospital papers and bills. Finally she found the one the doctor had signed to release her. There it was, Dr. Jeff Madia.

She couldn't believe it. "This cannot be true," she said to herself aloud.

Just then Sophia called up to Litsa, "I think this is your doctor coming up the driveway."

Stopping at the mirror to smooth her hair, she hurried down the stairs with care, not knowing what to expect. Sophia was at the door and Litsa peered over her shoulder waiting for the truck to come to a stop. The doctor got out of the truck and began walking toward the front porch. Litsa couldn't believe her eyes. She held her breath hoping this time it was not a dream.

"Excuse me, Mother," she said, edging around Sophia and out the door. She stepped to the edge of the porch to meet him and, with tears in her eyes, looked deeply into his. In one motion he was up on the porch and holding her in his arms as he whispered in her ear, "My darling Litsa, I will never leave you again." This time it was no dream.

About The Author

Verla Clemens was born in Colorado and has traveled extensively throughout the west. In her early stories the sites she depicts are geographically accurate though most of her characters are fictional. She is currently preparing two more books for publication.

Sandra Kruger editor and co-writer is a native of Arizona, and has lived in several western states and enjoys hiking in the mountains of Colorado. Both Verla and Sandra are avid horse lovers. Sandra has been writing with Verla Clemens for two years, but their friendship extends far beyond that.

Printed in the United States
20744LVS00007B/184